EGMONT
We bring stories to life

First published in Great Britain in 2020 by Egmont Books UK Ltd
2 Minster Court, 10th floor, London EC3R 7BB
www.egmont.com

Written by Brenda Apsley
Designed by Jeannette OToole for Ruby Shoes Limited
Cover Designed by John Stuckey

This book is an original creation of Egmont Books UK Ltd

Parental guidance is advised for all craft and colouring activities. Always ask an adult to help when using glue, paint and scissors. Wear protective clothing and cover surfaces to avoid staining.

Stay safe online. Egmont is not responsible for content hosted by third parties.

Egmont takes its responsibility to the planet and its inhabitants very seriously. We aim to use papers from well-managed forests run by responsible suppliers.

ISBN 978 1 4052 9900 8
71152/001
Printed in Italy

This
POWER RANGERS
BEAST MORPHERS
ANNUAL belongs to

_____

_____

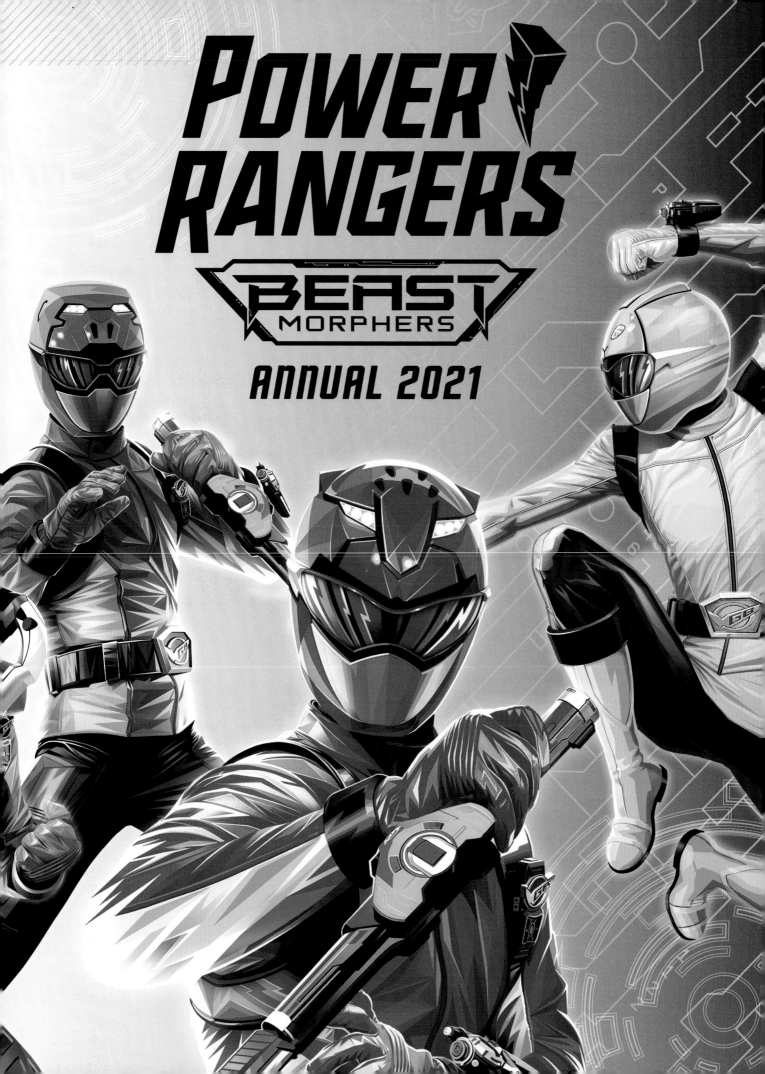

CONTENTS

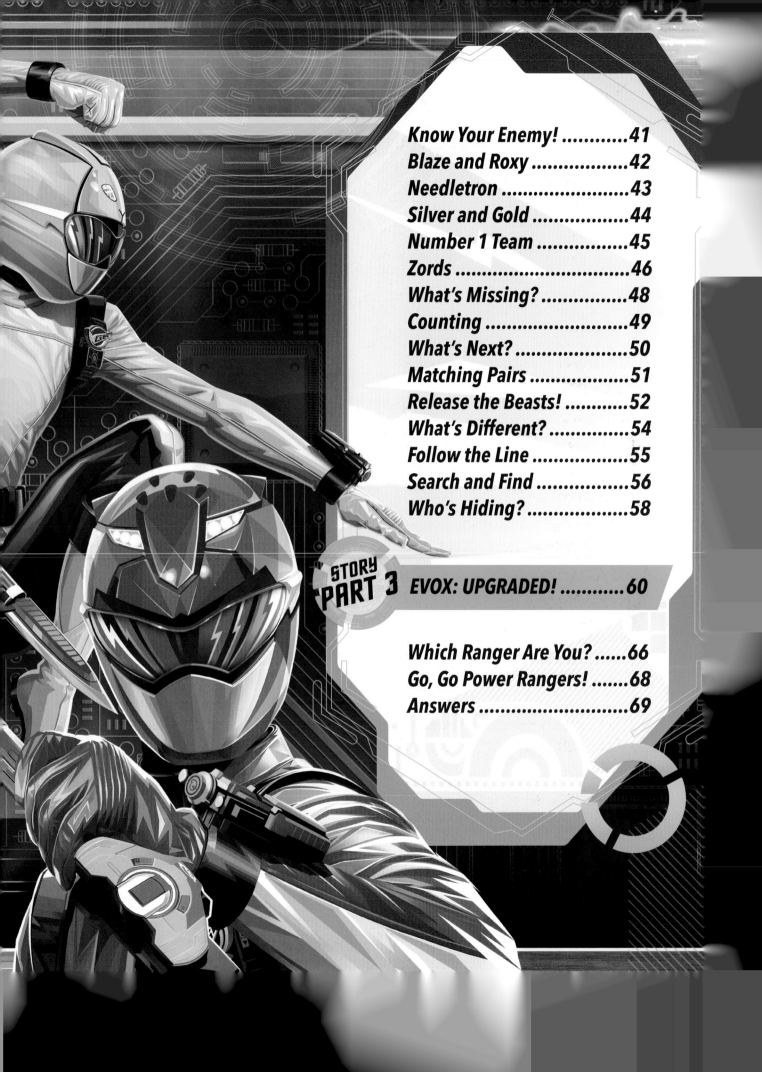

Coral Harbour was about to switch to a new, clean energy: MORPH-X.

BEASTS ... UNLEASHED!

Blaze and Devon were practising karate when Mayor Daniels, Devon's dad, came to collect him.

When Mayor Daniels was driven to Grid Battleforce, Devon snuck in behind him.

Commander Shaw and chief scientist Nate Silva explained Morph-X.

"It's pure energy," said Nate. "I've made it into a liquid and tapped into the Power Rangers Morphin Grid. We'll have access to the most powerful energy source EVER."

"Mistake," said the mayor. "Someone will try to take it – and you won't be able to stop them."

Devon got into the lab as Commander Shaw arrived with his dad, so Devon hid ... and listened.

"This computer controls the system," said Nate. "The Morph-X combines with **animal DNA,** and humans mutate into ..."

"POWER RANGERS," said the mayor.

"Correct," said Commander Shaw. "Our top cadets, **BLAZE**, **RAVI** and **ROXY**."

"We've got special equipment," said Nate. "Beast-X Blasters, Sabers, Morphers and Morph-X Keys. And these **transporters send anything ... anywhere.**"

"If someone comes for the Morph-X, we'll be ready," said Shaw.

Devon watched **Blaze**, **Ravi** and **Roxy**, but when he saw a huge SNAKE he jumped, and knocked over equipment: CLANG!

Security men led Devon away. "Wait!" he cried. "There's a **snake avatar** virus thing in your computer." But the guards ignored him.

Minutes later, "Immobilising cadets," Nate told Shaw. "And I checked. **No virus detected**."

Outside, Mayor Daniels made a speech. "Today we tap into a source of clean energy," he said. "The future is ...

MORPH-X!"

In the lab, Shaw said, "Activate the Morphin Grid," and liquid flowed into the cadets, but then ...

BEEP! BEEP! BEEP! sounded an alarm, and a voice said,

"I AM EVOX. THE MORPHIN GRID WILL BE MINE!"

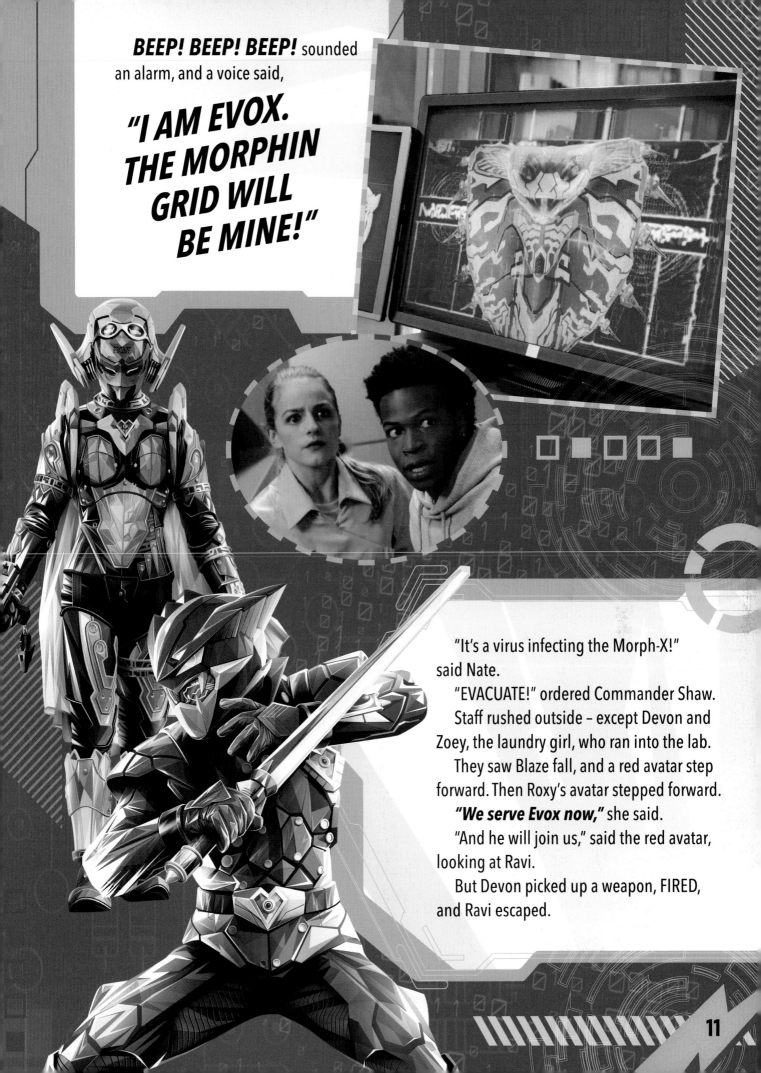

"It's a virus infecting the Morph-X!" said Nate.

"EVACUATE!" ordered Commander Shaw.

Staff rushed outside – except Devon and Zoey, the laundry girl, who ran into the lab.

They saw Blaze fall, and a red avatar step forward. Then Roxy's avatar stepped forward.

"We serve Evox now," she said.

"And he will join us," said the red avatar, looking at Ravi.

But Devon picked up a weapon, FIRED, and Ravi escaped.

Devon, Zoey and Ravi fought the avatars until **black tentacles** wrapped around them.

Nate fired a blast that destroyed the tentacles, then, "Morph sequence," he said, as Ravi morphed into …
BLUE RANGER.

But who would replace Blaze and Roxy as **POWER RANGERS?**
DEVON and **ZOEY!**

RED RANGER
had the
speed of a cheetah

YELLOW RANGER
had the
agility of a jackrabbit

BLUE RANGER
had the
strength of a gorilla

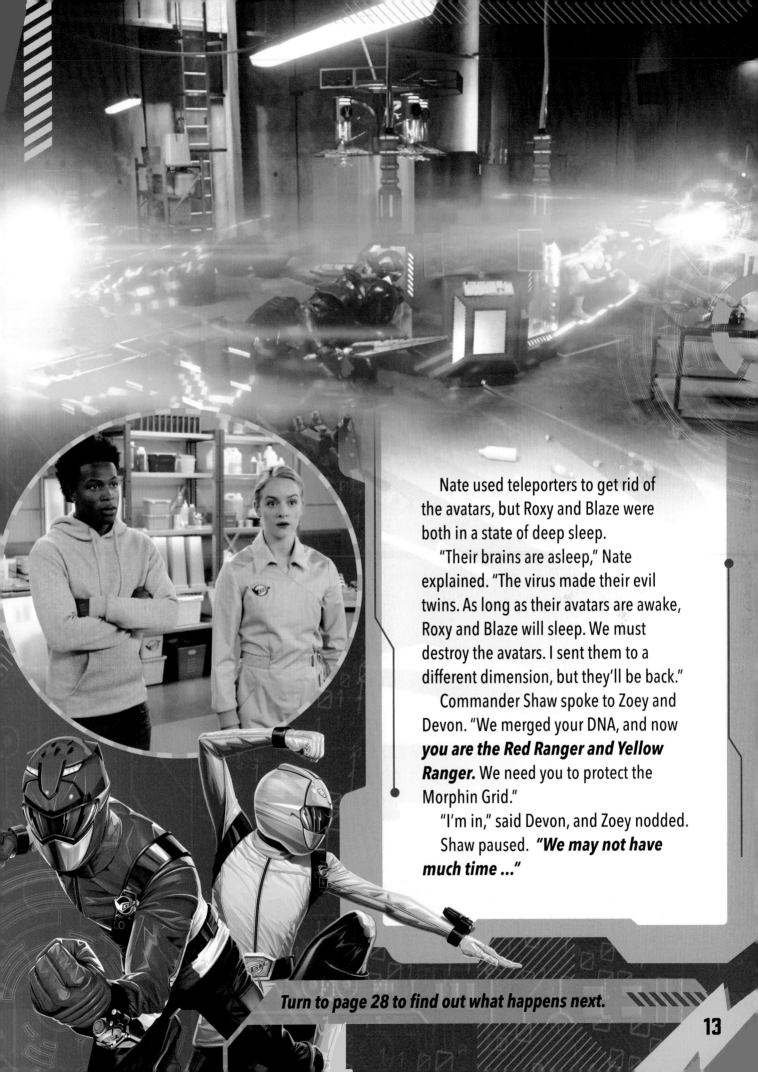

Nate used teleporters to get rid of the avatars, but Roxy and Blaze were both in a state of deep sleep.

"Their brains are asleep," Nate explained. "The virus made their evil twins. As long as their avatars are awake, Roxy and Blaze will sleep. We must destroy the avatars. I sent them to a different dimension, but they'll be back."

Commander Shaw spoke to Zoey and Devon. "We merged your DNA, and now *you are the Red Ranger and Yellow Ranger.* We need you to protect the Morphin Grid."

"I'm in," said Devon, and Zoey nodded.

Shaw paused. *"We may not have much time ..."*

Turn to page 28 to find out what happens next.

RED RANGER

RED RANGER is a born leader.

"ENEMIES? Bring 'em on!"

CIVILIAN NAME: Devon
MORPH-X DNA: Cheetah
SPECIAL SKILLS: Super speed

Where Red Ranger leads, others follow!

When Blaze, the original Red Ranger prospect, was turned into an evil avatar, Devon took his place.

He loves martial arts workouts, gaming – and playing tricks and pranks on people.

"Hey, all's fair in life and gaming, huh?"

14

RED RANGER WEAPONS:

- ✪ CHEETAH CLAWS
- ✪ BEAST-X BLASTER AND BLADE
- ✪ CHEETAH BEAST BLASTER

RED RANGER BEAST RACER ZORDS:

- ✪ BATTLE MODE
- ✪ CHEETAH MODE
- ✪ REMOTE MODE

RED RANGER BEAST BOT: CRUISE!

Cruise becomes a motorbike and Red Ranger's Battle Zord.
He is fast, loyal and strong.

ODD ONE OUT

To be a Ranger you need a great eye for detail!

Look carefully – which Yellow Ranger is different? Tick ✔ the odd one out.

a ✔

b ✔

c ✔

d ✔

e ✔

16

Answers on page 69

CRUISE

Cruise is Red Ranger's super-fast Beast Bot.

1

2

3

4

5

6

7

8

9

Which 3 picture pieces fit together to make Cruise?
Write the numbers below.

BLUE RANGER

BLUE RANGER is a smart, disciplined and no-nonsense hacker.

"RULES are there to be followed, right?"

CIVILIAN NAME: Ravi
MORPH-X DNA: Gorilla
SPECIAL SKILLS: Super-strength

Blue Ranger is serious, and always plays by the rules.

Ravi trained hard to become the Blue Ranger. He is super-strong thanks to his gorilla DNA.

"The job ALWAYS comes first!"

BLUE RANGER WEAPONS:

✪ *BEAST-X BLASTER*
✪ *BEAST-X BLADE*

BLUE RANGER BEAST WHEELER ZORDS:

✪ *GORILLA MODE*
✪ *REMOTE MODE*

BLUE RANGER BEAST BOT: SMASH!

Smash punches his way through enemies with his two huge fists. He's a little bit goofy, and likes hugs.

IT'S A MATCH!

Look carefully – can you find the exact match for Blue Ranger?

Answers on page 69

WHICH BEAST BOT?

Follow the lines to work out which line connects Nate with Jax.

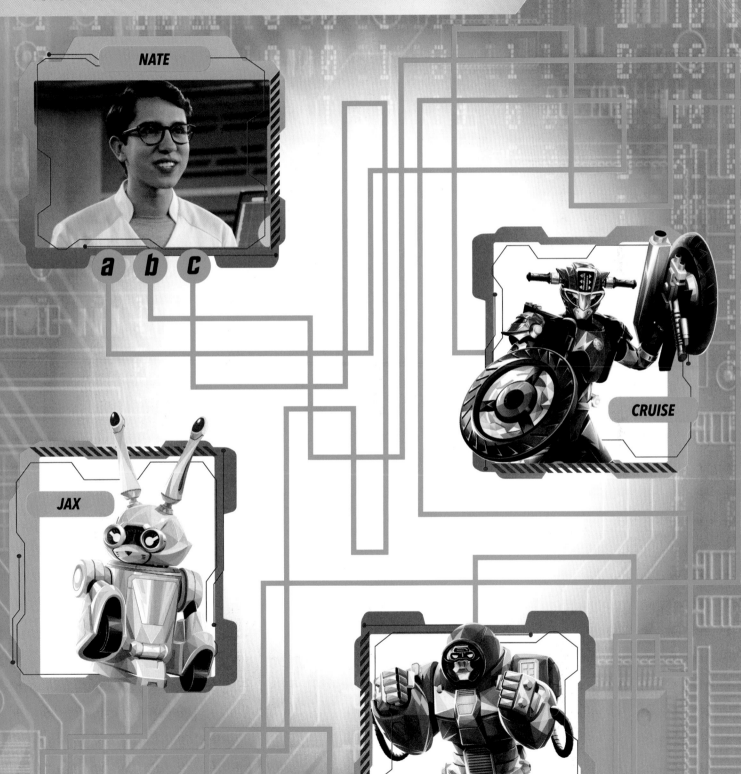

NATE

a b c

CRUISE

JAX

SMASH

Answers on page 69

YELLOW RANGER

YELLOW RANGER is super-agile.

"Time off is wasted time!"

CIVILIAN NAME: Zoey
MORPH-X DNA: Jackrabbit
SPECIAL SKILLS: High jumps and kicks

Yellow Ranger is brave, and always tries to do what's right.

Zoey became the Yellow Ranger after Roxy was put into a coma.

She helps at a recycling centre, teaches yoga – and makes great carrot smoothies.

"It's important to do what's RIGHT!"

YELLOW RANGER WEAPONS:

✪ *BEAST-X BLASTER*
✪ *BEAST-X BLADE*

YELLOW RANGER BEAST CHOPPER ZORDS:

✪ *JACKRABBIT MODE*
✪ *REMOTE MODE*

YELLOW RANGER BEAST BOT: JAX!

Jax helps Zoey to be the best she can be, and gives her carrots for energy.

STAND TOGETHER

The Power Rangers are under attack. They need to re-group so they can fight as a TEAM.

The Yellow Ranger and the Blue Ranger need to get to the Red Ranger. Can you guide them through the maze to reach him?

START

FINISH

Answers on page 69

GOLD RANGER

GOLD RANGER *is super-smart, and full of ideas.*

CIVILIAN NAME: Nate
MORPH-X DNA: Mantis
SPECIAL SKILLS: Martial arts master

Gold Ranger built the Beast Bots and Zords for the Power Rangers.

Nate joined Grid Battleforce at age 6 to work on merging animal DNA and artificial intelligence. Now he's head of technology.

GOLD RANGER WEAPON:

✪ STRIKER SABER

GOLD RANGER GEAR:

✪ BEAST WRECKER ZORD
✪ STRIKER MORPHER

SILVER RANGER

SILVER RANGER *is extremely loyal.*

CIVILIAN NAME: Steel
MORPH-X DNA: Scarab
SPECIAL SKILLS: Super-strength

Steel was created by Nate and is half human and half robot. He is loyal, and has amazing strength. He's also stubborn, and not too bright. Nate thinks of Steel as the brother he never had.

SILVER RANGER WEAPON:
- ✪ STRIKER SABER

SILVER RANGER GEAR:
- ✪ BEAST JET ZORD
- ✪ STRIKER MORPHER

EVOX'S REVENGE

The avatars transported from the lab. "Where are we?" asked Roxy.

A figure with glowing green eyes had the answer. "In the CYBER DIMENSION. I'm Scrozzle and these," he said as armed soldiers appeared, "are my TRONICS. Now bow down to me!"

In a flash of energy a huge cobra loomed over them. It spat flames from its eyes that turned the Tronics into dust.

"**YOU** BOW DOWN TO **ME!**" said the cobra. "**I MUST GET OUT OF THIS DIMENSION.**"

"I have a teleporter," said Scrozzle. "But only enough Morph-X to transport avatars."

"GO," said the cobra. "GET ME MORE MORPH-X. **DO NOT FAIL.**"

In a flash, Blaze and Scrozzle were gone.

At Grid Battleforce, Commander Shaw had things to show the Rangers.

"Our own robots?" asked Devon.

"I prefer **Beast Bots,**" said Nate. "Infused with animal DNA."

"I'm **Jax**," the yellow Beast Bot told Zoey. "To make you fast."

"I'm **Smash**, and I like ... hugs," said Ravi's blue Beast Bot.

Cruise, Devon's red Beast Bot, said hi by turning into a motorcycle.

Zoey spoke for all three: "Incredible!"

Commander Shaw was about to name the team leader (and her son Ravi hoped it would be him) when alarms sounded. "Security breach at Morph-X centre."

Outside, Scrozzle and Blaze were stealing Morph-X.

"Meet my new friends," said Blaze as Tronics attacked, but the friends soon outfought them.

Scrozzle had another plan. "I'll charge the EVOX virus with Morph-X to make a ROBOTRON!" he said, transforming a stack of black tyres into a huge beast fighter: CYCLOTRON!

"MORPHIN TIME!" cried the friends.

"ACTIVATE BEAST POWER!" and the Power Rangers appeared.

"UNLEASH THE BEAST!"

"TRANSFORM! BEAST-X SABERS!"

Leaving the Tronics to face the Rangers, Scrozzle and Blaze left with the Morph-X ...

The fight was hard, but the Rangers were on top until ... Red Ranger froze when he saw a dog, Blue attacked Yellow, and Yellow's energy was gone. "Something weird is happening to us," Red Ranger told Nate.

Nate couldn't explain it, but Devon had an idea ...

"You two argue," he told Zoey and Ravi. "We need to work together, because *we're stronger as a TEAM.*"

In the Cyber Dimension, Scrozzle used Morph-X to power a giant GIGADRONE robot, but Devon was waiting for it at Grid Battleforce. **"ACTIVATE BEAST POWER,"** he ordered. **"ACTIVATE BATTLE MODE."**

Towering over the city, the two giants fought ... until Devon saw a dog poster, and froze again.

Nate worked out the problem. "The EVOX virus caused your weaknesses," he explained. "It's being merged with animal DNA: Zoey needs **carrots** for her jackrabbit energy, Ravi's gorilla DNA sent him **wild** – and when Devon saw the **dog** poster he froze, like a cheetah."

Now the Power Rangers **attacked as a TEAM** until ...

"Virus eliminated!" said Red Ranger.

"Rangers, your first mission was a success," Shaw told them. "And team leader will be ..."

"DEVON!" said Zoey and Ravi.

Find out what happens next on page 60.

SECRET CODE

Do you have what it takes to be a Power Ranger?
You need to know how to read secret messages.

1	2	3	4	5	6	7	8	9	10	11	12	13
S	T	U	V	W	X	Y	Z	A	B	C	D	E

14	15	16	17	18	19	20	21	22	23	24	25	26
F	G	H	I	J	K	L	M	N	O	P	Q	R

Decode this message by writing the correct letters underneath the numbers.

21 9 7   2 16 13

24 23 5 13 26   10 13

5 17 2 16   7 23 3

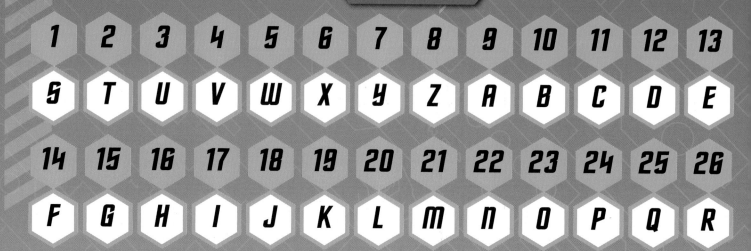

BADGE MATCH

Draw lines to match sets of 2 matching badges.

Which is the only badge that
does not have a match?
Draw and colour it here.

EVOX

EVOX is an EVIL, cruel virus.

"The Morphin Grid will be mine!"

Evox is trapped in the Cyber Dimension as a cobra holograph. To escape, he needs enough Morph-X to make him real and have the energy to destroy the Power Rangers.

Evox can get into computer systems, and his cobra avatar shoots laser fire from its eyes!

THE TRONICS

The Tronics are an army of cloned fighters that obey their evil masters. They are teleported to where they are needed.

There are HUNDREDS of them: silent, strong and armed with laser-firing blasters.

SCROZZLE

The Tronics were made by Scrozzle, an evil inventor. He uses his Robotrons to help Evox, Blaze and Roxy.

MEMORY TEST

Look at the pictures, then close this book.
Whose pictures can you remember?

SILVER RANGER

GOLD RANGER

EVOX

YELLOW RANGER

RED RANGER

CRUISE

JAX

ROXY

BLUE RANGER

Did you get all 10?
WELL DONE.

SMASH

NO RANGER STANDS ALONE

BE THE BEST!

"LAUNCH CRUISE BATTLE MODE!"

KNOW YOUR ENEMY!

The Power Rangers can defeat super-powerful enemies when they work together as a TEAM.

Put your ENEMY ID SKILLS to the test!

1 Can you NAME this enemy?

_____

2 Tick ✔ the boxes that are missing from this picture.

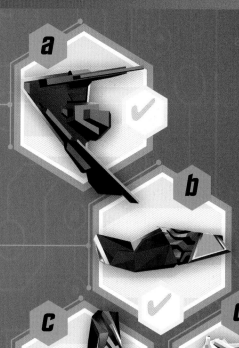

a ✔

b ✔

c ✔

d ✔

Answers on page 69

BLAZE

When Blaze was infected by a virus Evox took control of him. He moves from the Cyber Dimension to steal Morph-X for his master.

"As you wish, Evox!"

ROXY

The virus that infected Roxy changed her into a cold, hard villain. Now her only loyalty is to Evox.

"We serve Evox!"

NEEDLETRON

When Blaze went to steal Morph-X from X-bikes, he infected a bicycle pump. Result? Needletron, a Robotron with a fighting needle for a right hand, and an arm that fires deadly blasts.

"I LIKE IT, STRAIGHT TO THE POINT!"

SILVER AND GOLD

Use the small pictures to help you colour in the Gold Ranger, Nate, and the Silver Ranger, Steel.

GOLD RANGER

SILVER RANGER

NUMBER 1 TEAM

Which 3 jigsaw pieces complete the Number 1 Team?

a

b

c

d

e

f **g**

h

Answers on page 69

ZORDS

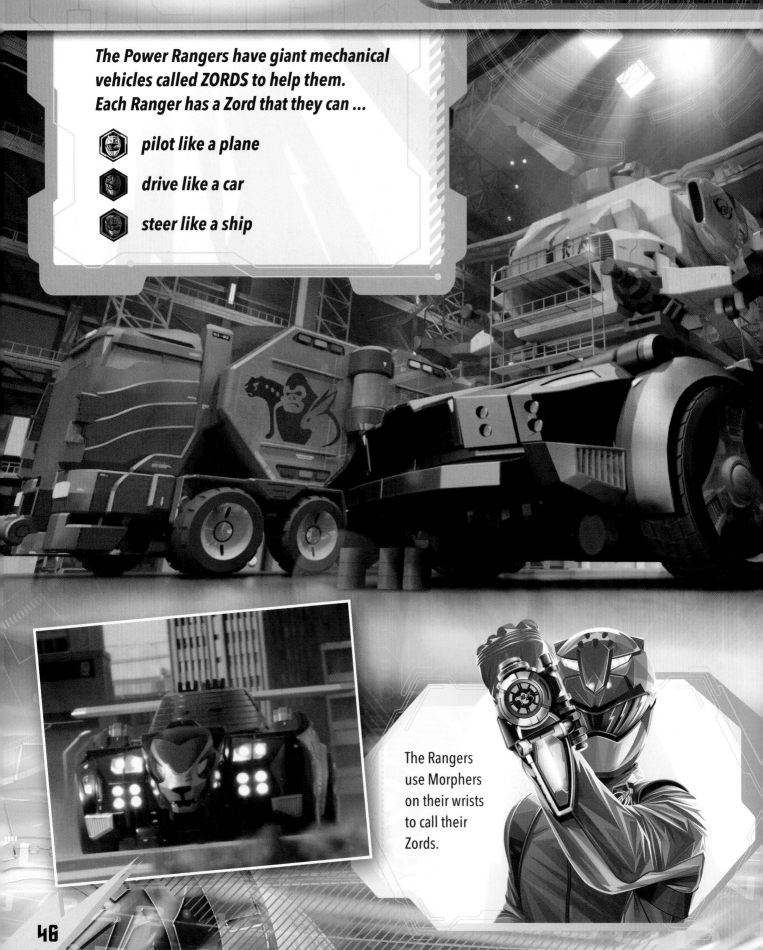

The Power Rangers have giant mechanical vehicles called ZORDS to help them. Each Ranger has a Zord that they can ...

- pilot like a plane
- drive like a car
- steer like a ship

The Rangers use Morphers on their wrists to call their Zords.

To fight super-sized villains, the Power Rangers need super-sized and super-powerful fighting machines. How well do you know your Zords?

Question:
Put together the Red, Blue and Yellow Zords, and what do you get?

Answer:

_ _ _ _ _ _ _ _ _ _ _**ZORD,**

a huge humanoid robot fighter.

Question:
What do you get if you combine the Red, Blue, Yellow, Silver and Gold Zords?

Answer:

_ _ _ _ _ _ _ _ _ _ _**ZORD,**

the ultimate TEAM player.

Answers on page 69

WHAT'S MISSING?

The Power Rangers have their own animal DNA.

RED RANGER

CHEETAH

YELLOW RANGER

JACKRABBIT

BLUE RANGER

GORILLA

Draw pictures in the blank squares so that the CHEETAH, GORILLA and JACKRABBIT appear *only once* in each line going across → and down ↓

Answers on page 69

COUNTING

The Tronics are always ready to fight for their evil masters.
How many can you count?

Answers on page 69

WHAT'S NEST?

What comes next in each line? Draw in the missing pictures to finish the patterns!

Test your Power Ranger puzzle solving skills!

1

2

3

4

Answers on page 69

MATCHING PAIRS

Draw lines to join up the matching pairs.
The first one is done for you.

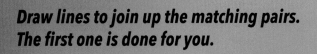

How many pairs? Circle the number:

1 2 3 4 5 6 7 8

Answers on page 69

RELEASE THE BEASTS!

The Rangers need their Beast Bots! Crack the maze by using your pencils to guide Jax to the Yellow Ranger, Smash to the Blue Ranger and Cruise to the Red Ranger.

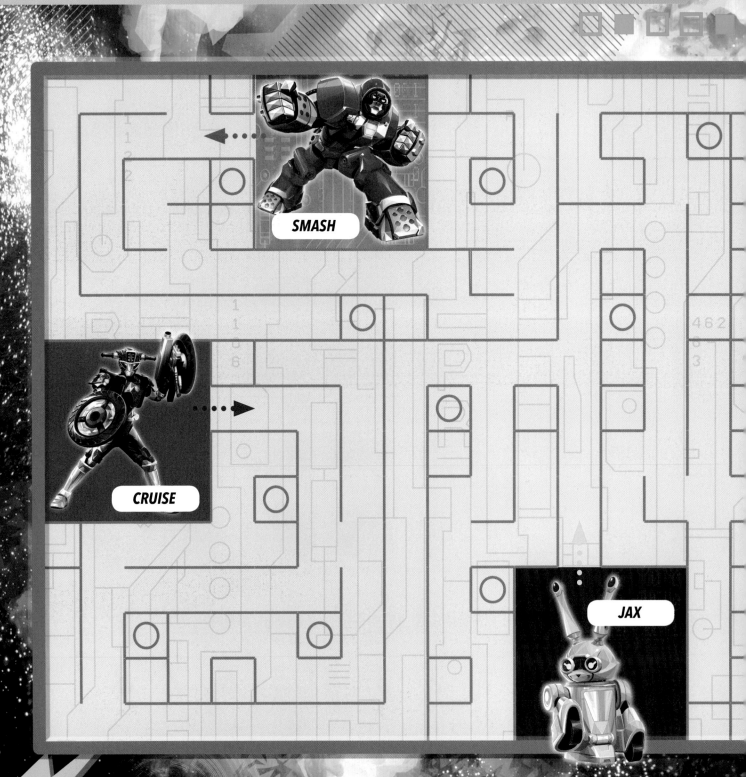

SMASH

CRUISE

JAX

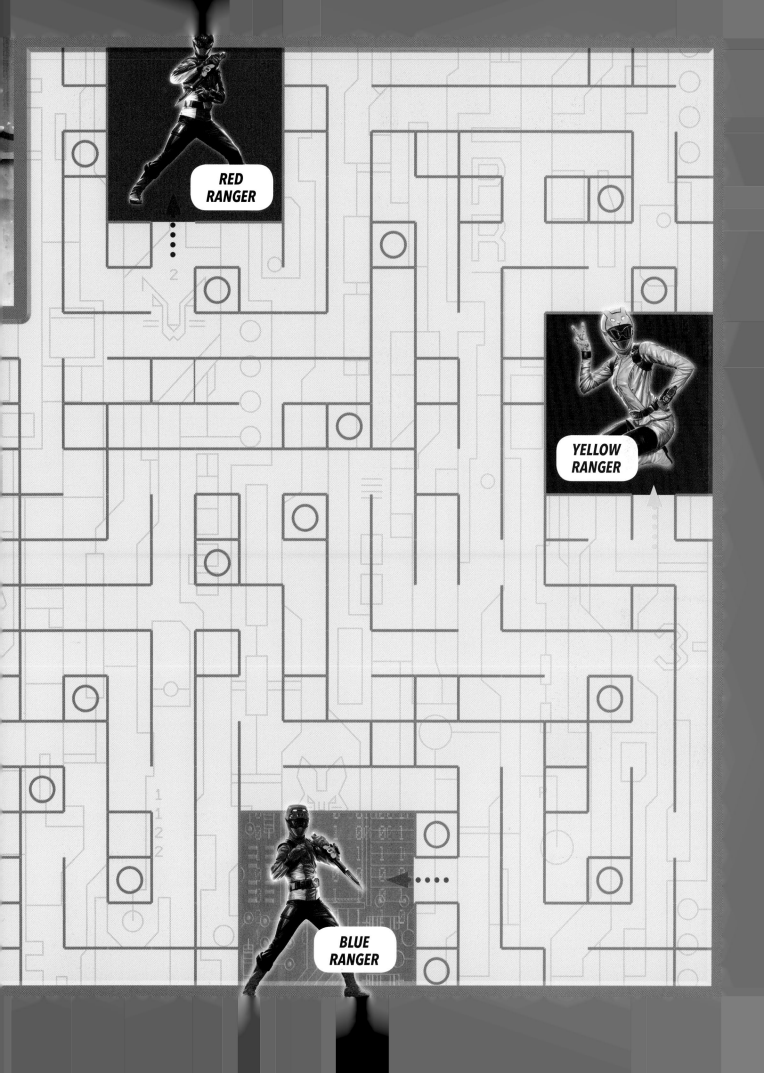

WHAT'S DIFFERENT?

These pictures of Ultrazord look the same, but 8 things are different in picture 2. Can you spot them all?

54

Answers on page 69

FOLLOW THE LINE

Where is Ultrazord trying to get to?
Follow the line to find out.

CORAL HARBOUR

GRID BATTLEFORCE

CYBER DIMENSION

Answers on page 69

5

SEARCH AND FIND

Use the grid to pin point the coordinates of the Rangers and their enemies! Then add them to the key at the side.

The Power Rangers need to know where their allies and enemies are at all times!

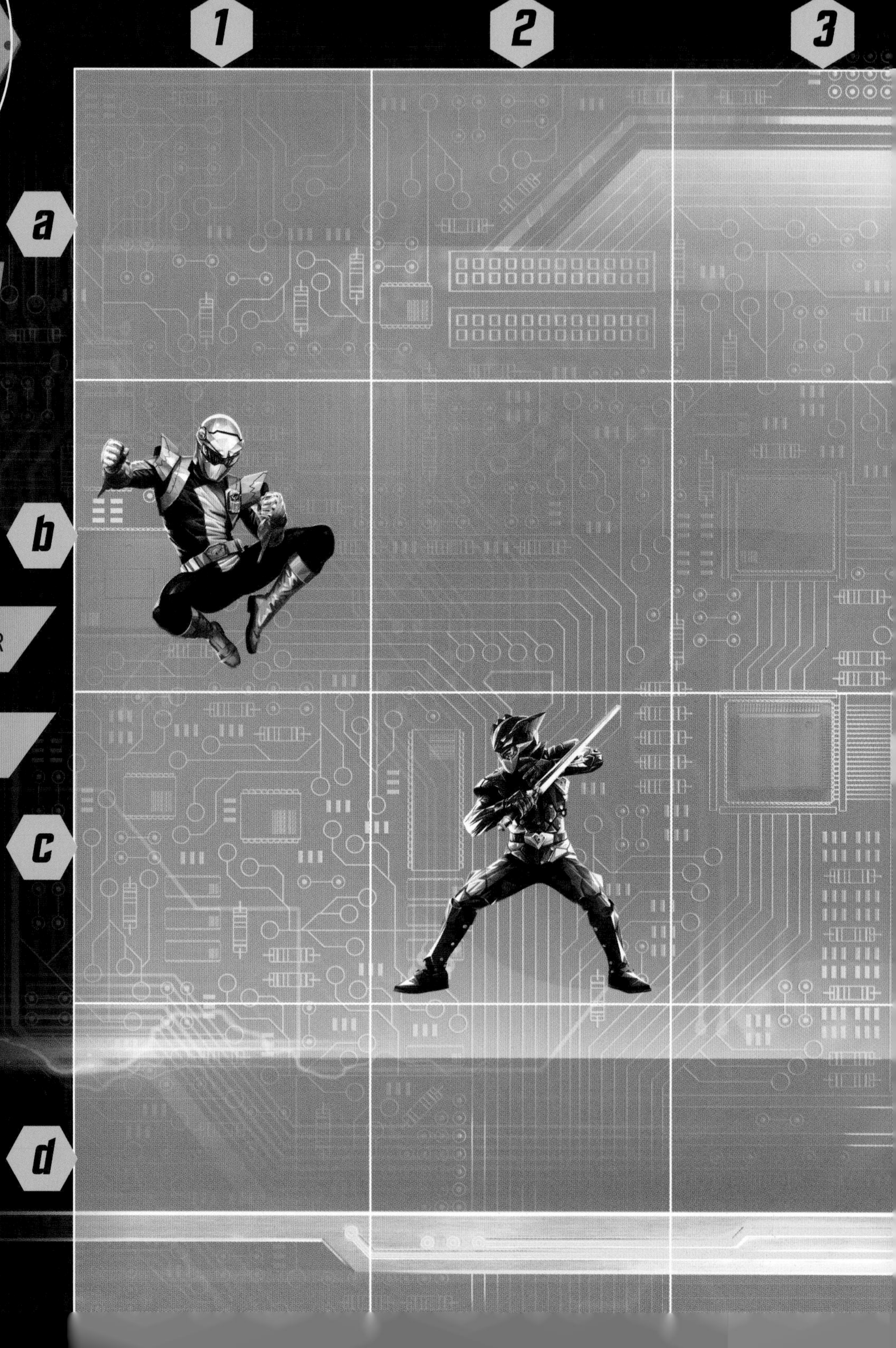

1 **b** SILVER RANGER

GOLD RANGER

EVOX

BLAZE

ROXY

TRONIC

1   **2**   **3**

a

b

c

d

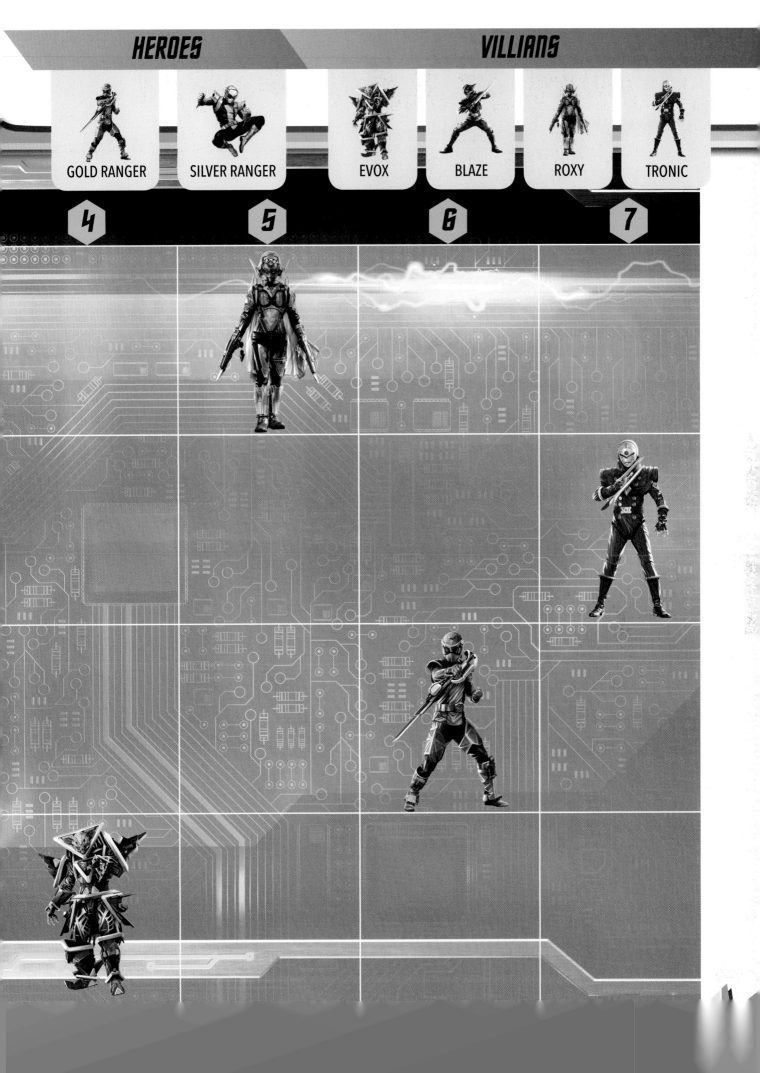

HEROES | VILLIANS

GOLD RANGER | SILVER RANGER | EVOX | BLAZE | ROXY | TRONIC

4 | 5 | 6 | 7

WHO'S HIDING?

SMOKE! FLAMES! EXPLOSIONS!
In the heat of battle it's hard
to see your enemies and allies.

1

2

3

4

Can you identify these heroes and villains from their shadows?

YELLOW RANGER

ULTRAZORD

ROXY

BLAZE

5

6

8

7

EVOX

BLUE
RANGER

MEGAZORD

RED
RANGER

Answers on page 69

STORY PART 3 — EVOX: UPGRADED!

In the Cyber Dimension Scrozzle was creating a new body for Evox so he could escape, and take over the Morphin Grid.

At Grid Battleforce The Rangers had to defend the Morph-X storage tower, but Devon had been captured, and was being held by Tronics in the Cyber Dimension.

Nate had made a Cyber Gate, a portal to take them into the Cyber Dimension so they could rescue Devon. But they needed extra big and extra strong help to defeat the evil villains.

"*ULTRAZORD*," said Nate. "It's all our ZORDS combined. If that isn't powerful enough, nothing is."

Piece by piece, Ultrazord took shape, until ...

"BEAST ... UNLEASHED!"

"Deploy Beast-X Ultrazord!" ordered Commander Shaw, and the huge fighting machine loomed over the city.

Deep in the Cyber Dimension Ultrazord appeared on Scrozzle's computer screen. "The Rangers are here, with a crazy new Zord combo!" he said.

"Send an army of Gigadrones," Blaze's evil avatar told him. "Tear those fools apart!"

That started the battle to end all battles, until ...

"BEAST -X ULTRA STRIKE!"

and the Gigadrones were blasted into tiny pieces. A MILLION tiny pieces.

Evox transformed from a cobra to a towering humanoid form. **_"FINALLY I'M FREE!"_** he said, facing Ultrazord and the Rangers and firing sheets of vicious, super-powerful red flames.

Evox's attack destroyed Ultrazord, but the Rangers were safe, and they found Devon, who had escaped in the chaos.

But Nate's news was bad: "Our Zords are history."

Evox appeared again. "No escape," he said. "You're finished."

Devon didn't buy that. **_"ACTIVATE BEAST POWER!"_** he cried. **_"UNLEASH THE BEAST!"_**

When Evox attacked again the Rangers were in trouble. BIG trouble.

"I am unstoppable!" said Evox. "Time to leave this dimension."

He began to teleport to get to the Morph-X tower at Coral Harbour, but Red Ranger and Cruise managed to get away. They planned to destroy the tower and its contents before Evox got to it.

But to do that they first had to defeat Blaze and his new Zord ...

Nate took over Scrozzle's computer and Evox's teleport sequence stuttered, then stopped: **_"TERMINATED."_**

"What's happening?" said Evox. Teleporting was his only way to escape from the Cyber Dimension. **"NOOOOO!"** he cried, as he was covered in swirls of green smoke ... then disappeared.

Evox was **GONE!**

The Rangers ran back through the Cyber Gate into Grid Battleforce. But where were Red Ranger and Cruise?

The team watched as smoke billowed, cleared – and their friends stepped to safety.

"Good to be back," said Devon.

Roxy had already woken from her sleep state, and soon after, Blaze woke up, too. The REAL ROXY and BLAZE were back, and safe!

Job done, the team got together to share their success.

"You showed trust, loyalty and courage, but key to your teamwork is ... FRIENDSHIP," Mayor Daniels told them. "It saved our city, and I'm proud to give you these Coral Harbour Medals of Valour."

The whole Power Rangers TEAM posed for a smiling group selfie.

"CHEESE!"

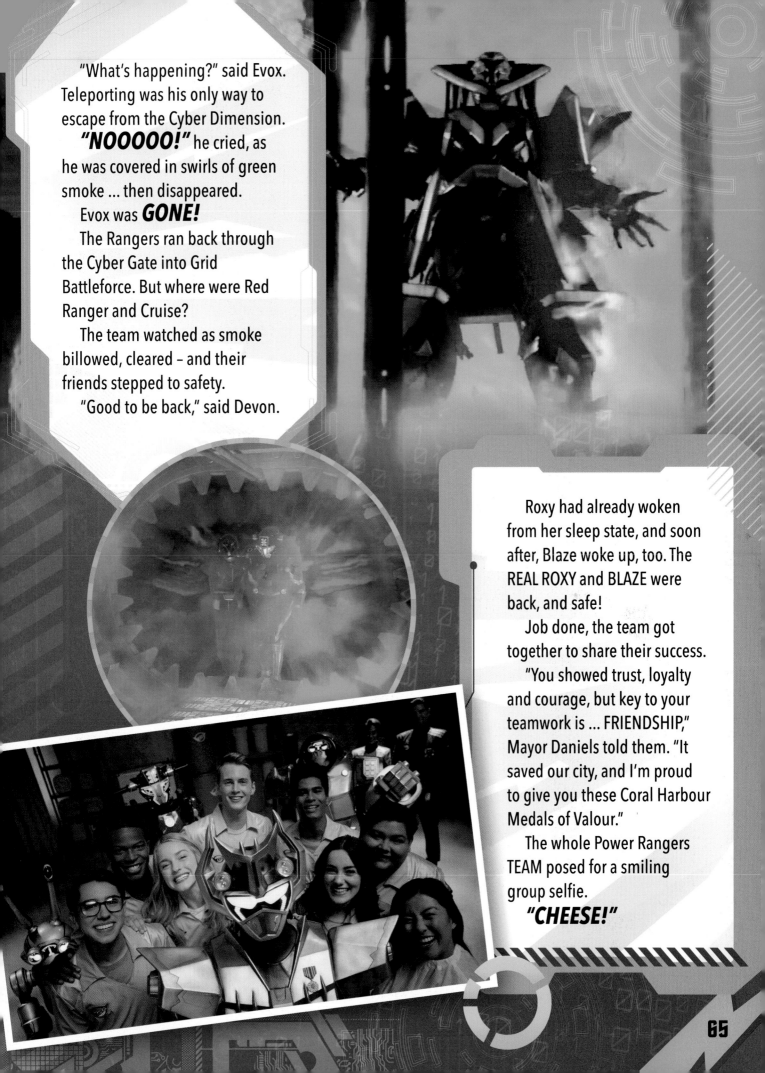

WHICH RANGER ARE YOU?

Which Power Ranger are you most like? For each question, tick ✔ answer A, B or C.

The Power Rangers work as a TEAM with a mix of lots of different strengths and skills!

1 PHYSICAL STRENGTHS

You love yoga and carrot smoothies. **A** ✔

You really care about diet and exercise. **C** ✔

You're a martial arts master. **B** ✔

2 PERSONALITY

You always play by the rules. **C** ✔

You want to make the world a better place. **A** ✔

You're a born leader. **B** ✔

3 ANIMAL AFFINITY

Grrr! You love big cats. **B** ✔

Jackrabbit high kicks are fun! **A** ✔

You think apes can teach us a lot. **C** ✔

4

TIME OFF

What time off? Never happens! **A** ✓

Your number 1 like? Gaming. **B** ✓

Time off? I prefer training! **C** ✓

5

ANNOYING HABITS

You can be TOO serious. **C** ✓

You play pranks and tricks. **B** ✓

You never take a rest. **A** ✓

Count the letters you ticked, and write the number of each: **A** **B** **C**

If you scored mostly As you are most like ZOEY:

YELLOW RANGER —

you are kind, caring, agile and very hard-working.

If you scored mostly Bs you are most like DEVON:

RED RANGER —

you are super-fit, a top games master and a joker.

If you scored mostly Cs you are most like RAVI:

BLUE RANGER —

you are serious, smart, reliable and super-strong.

GO GO POWER RANGERS

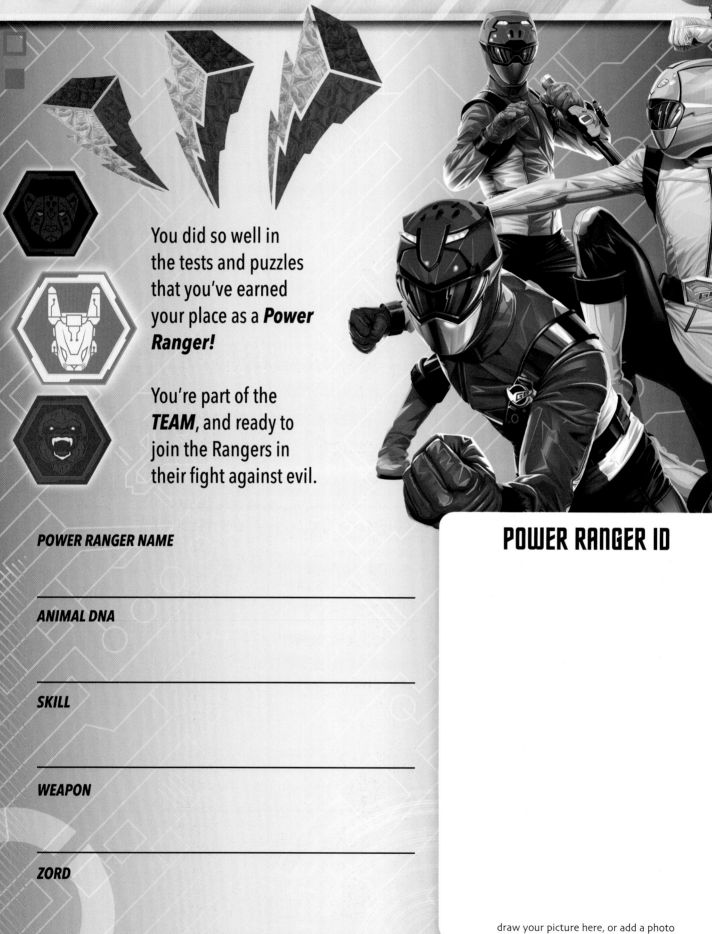

You did so well in the tests and puzzles that you've earned your place as a *Power Ranger!*

You're part of the *TEAM*, and ready to join the Rangers in their fight against evil.

POWER RANGER NAME

_____

ANIMAL DNA

_____

SKILL

_____

WEAPON

_____

ZORD

_____

POWER RANGER ID

draw your picture here, or add a photo

ANSWERS

PAGE 16 ODD ONE OUT
Picture d is the odd one out

PAGE 17 CRUISE

PAGE 20 IT'S A MATCH!
Picture 3 is an exact match

PAGE 21 WHICH BEAST BOT?
Line b connects to Jax

PAGE 24-25 STAND TOGETHER

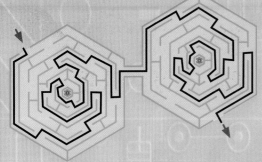

PAGE 32 SECRET CODE
MAY THE POWER BE WITH YOU

PAGE 33 BADGE MATCH
This badge has no match

PAGE 41 KNOW YOUR ENEMY!
1. Evox
2. Part A and Part C

PAGE 45 NUMBER 1 TEAM
Jigsaw pieces b, e and g

PAGE 46-47 ZORDS
MEGAZORD
ULTRAZORD

PAGE 48 WHAT'S MISSING?

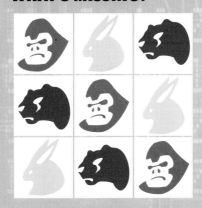

PAGE 49 COUNTING
There are 12 Tronics

PAGE 50 WHAT'S NEXT?

PAGE 51 MATCHING PAIRS
There are 7 pairs

PAGE 52-53 RELEASE THE BEASTS!

PAGE 54 WHAT'S DIFFERENT?

PAGE 55 FOLLOW THE LINE
ULTRAZORD is trying to reach
Coral Harbour

PAGE 56-57 SEARCH AND FIND
1 b   SILVER RANGER
6 c   GOLD RANGER
4 d   EVOX
2 c   BLAZE
5 a   ROXY
7 b   TRONIC

PAGE 58-59 WHO'S HIDING?
1 – Megazord
2 – Yellow Ranger
3 – Blue Ranger
4 – Roxy
5 – Ultrazord
6 – Blaze
7 – Red Ranger
8 – Evox